Usborne
Illustrated
Stories
from the Greek
Myths

Contents

The
Wooden
Horse

Retold by
Russell Punter

Illustrated by
Matteo Pincelli

Contents

The costumes and buildings in this
version of the story come from
Classical Greece (c.500-400 B.C.),
the most popular setting for the tale.
The original story took place at the time
of the Mycenaeans – Greek people
who lived around 1600-1100 B.C.

Chapter 1

The runaway queen

Helen gazed out from the balcony of the royal palace. The passers-by below looked up in admiration. Like everyone who saw her, they thought she was the most beautiful woman in the world.

Helen led a life of luxury. But she wasn't happy.

Helen was married to King Menelaus of Sparta. He was proud of his lovely wife, and told her so every day.

"I want you to stay by my side forever," he would say. Helen never dared tell him how she felt.

One day, a young prince named Paris came to the palace. He was from the city of Troy, across the Aegean Sea. He had come to arrange the release of his aunt, who was being held prisoner by the Greeks.

When Paris met Helen, he fell
madly in love. "Come back to
Troy with me," he begged her,
one moonlit night.

Helen had fallen for Paris too.
So she agreed to go with him.

12

Menelaus was furious when he found out what had happened. His servants quivered in terror as he stomped around the throne room.

"Paris will pay for this!" he roared. "I don't care how long it takes, I'll get Helen back."

He immediately organized a meeting of all the kings of Greece.

Chapter 2

The Trojan war

Almost all the kings agreed to help bring Helen home. Only Odysseus, an experienced soldier and king of Ithaca, didn't want to go.

He had had enough of fighting, so he pretended to be crazy. Menelaus quickly saw through this ruse and Odysseus was forced to join the campaign whether he liked it or not.

The next morning, Menelaus, Odysseus and the other kings set sail with their army. Hundreds of ships crossed the sea to Troy.

Many days later, the Greek ships reached land. The soldiers waded ashore and stormed up the beach. The kings rode ahead of them in their golden chariots. Soon Troy was in their sights.

"Now all we have to do is get inside," said
Odysseus, who wanted to get home quickly.
But Troy was well defended.

Time and again, the Greeks attacked the mighty Trojan citadel.

But, however hard they tried, they couldn't break in. The Trojans were fierce fighters who defended their stronghold from every attack.

Despite this, the Greeks believed their enemy would crumble eventually. Little did they know just how long the war was set to last.

Over ten long years, a thousand ships brought more soldiers across the Aegean Sea. The roads to Troy became worn down by the marching hordes.

Many great warriors from both sides were killed as the years passed. But still the Trojans remained trapped in their own city. And the Greeks were still stuck outside, having gained no ground at all.

By now, the Greeks were beginning to give up.
"We'll never get in," they cried. "The walls of
Troy are impenetrable."

Then, one day, Odysseus had an idea. "It's pretty wild, and it'll take a lot of nerve," he announced. "But we might just pull it off."

Chapter 3

A big idea

The other Greek kings agreed to go along with the plan, so Odysseus took a large detachment of the army into the nearby forest, and ordered them to work, felling trees.

24

The Greek soldiers sawed the trees into planks and joined the planks together. Piece by piece, Odysseus's idea slowly took shape.

After days of hard work, the Greek army had built a mighty, magnificent...

...wooden horse.

Odysseus admired the men's efforts. The massive beast was even more imposing than he'd dared hope. The other Greek kings were equally impressed at what had been achieved.

"Now to put my plan into action," declared Odysseus confidently.

Chapter 4

Undercover

That night, the Greeks dragged the horse to the city gates. The huge creature was a colossal weight, but, little by little, the soldiers edged the result of all their hard work to the gates of Troy.

"Quietly now," whispered Odysseus, as they opened a small trap door in the horse's belly. Odysseus and some of his men climbed inside the hollow beast and closed the door behind them.

One soldier, named Sinon,
crouched down behind a
nearby rock and waited.

Meanwhile, King Menelaus and the other
Greeks went back to their ships and sailed out of
sight. The first part of the plan was complete.

30

The next morning, the Trojan guards couldn't believe their eyes when they looked outside.

"The Greeks have gone," cried one soldier.

"And there's a giant horse outside!" gasped another. "What on earth is going on?"

The Trojans ran out of the city and gazed in wonder at the new arrival.

It was time for Sinon to come out of hiding. "Who are you?" asked a soldier, raising his spear. "And what's this?"

"I ran away from the Greek army," lied Sinon. "They built the horse."

"But what's it for?" asked the soldier, staring up incredulously at the strange creature.

"It's a gift to the goddess Athene," explained Sinon, "to bring them luck on the trip home."

"Maybe it will bring us luck too," said the Trojan soldier. And he ordered that it be brought inside.

The troops hauled the creature into the city. Inside the wooden horse, Odysseus smiled to himself.

Chapter 5

The army awakes

The Trojans spent all day preparing a party to commemorate the end of the war. It was ten long years since they'd had anything so wonderful to celebrate.

The whole of Troy packed the streets. There was feasting, dancing and singing, and the celebrations lasted long into the night.

It was early morning before the Trojans eventually went to bed. Now, at last, Sinon could get to work.

He tiptoed across the square to the horse and tapped three times on its leg, quickly glancing back to make sure he hadn't woken the sleeping Trojans.

Inside, Odysseus leapt up. "That's the signal!" he whispered. He was ready to put the second part of his plan into action.

Gently, he opened the trap door, lowered a rope ladder to the ground and led his men out into the cool night air.

"Not a sound, men," breathed Odysseus to his troops. The Greek warriors scurried across the city as silently as they could.

The guards at the gates were fast asleep. Slowly, the Greek soldiers lifted off the wooden bolt and heaved open the doors. The rest of the Greek army was waiting outside.

"We're back as planned," said the leading soldier. "Right men," said Odysseus. "Now we attack!"

Chapter 6

The final battle

The Greek kings and their army stormed into the city. By the time the Trojans woke up and realized what was happening, it was too late. There was nothing to stop their enemies now.

The Greek soldiers crashed through the streets and houses in search of Menelaus's wife.

"Where's Helen?" they bellowed. "Give her up, you miserable Trojans!"

The Greeks stormed from place to place, ransacking the city as they went. The soldiers grabbed as much Trojan treasure as they could carry and killed anyone who got in their way.

Soon the city was ablaze, the flames
lighting up a scene of chaos and terror.

Paris rushed out to fight the Greeks.
But, realizing the Trojans were doomed
to defeat, he ran for his life.

He wasn't quick enough. An order from Menelaus sent an arrow flying through the air, and Paris fell to the ground.

"Now, where's Helen?" roared Menelaus.

Watching from above, Helen saw Paris struck down. The young Trojan was dead, and there was no possible escape for her.

"Perhaps Menelaus will throw me in prison," she thought anxiously. "Or kill me, like Paris. Any moment now, he'll find me."

Chapter 7

Return to Greece

Sure enough, it wasn't long before Helen was captured and brought before her husband. She trembled with fear about what might happen next.

Menelaus had been angry with his wife for ten years. He had planned to punish her, but the moment he saw her face, his rage disappeared.

"Welcome back, my love," he cried, his arms open wide. "You are forgiven."

"Finally," he sighed, "my beautiful wife is back by my side. Our mission here is over."

Helen was escorted back to the Greek ships, leaving the smoking ruins of Troy behind her.

As dawn broke, Menelaus, Odysseus, and the rest of the Greek army set sail, their vessels weighed down by Trojan treasure.

Helen didn't want to go back to Greece, but she had no choice. "At least I escaped with my life," she thought, as she sailed away.

Menelaus, meanwhile, stood on deck a happy man. At long last he was reunited with his queen, whose beauty had launched a thousand ships.

The Minotaur

Retold by
Russell Punter

Illustrated by
Linda Cavallini

Contents

The story of the Minotaur was first told about 3,000 years ago in Ancient Greece. Some people think that the idea for the Minotaur came from the sport of bull leaping that took place in Ancient Crete. In 1900, archeologists discovered underground storage passages on Crete. Perhaps they were the inspiration for the Labyrinth?

Chapter 1

A deadly demand

King Aegeus paced the floor of his
mighty palace at the heart of
Athens. He had been dreading this
day for the past nine years. As he
had expected, a messenger arrived
with a letter for him.

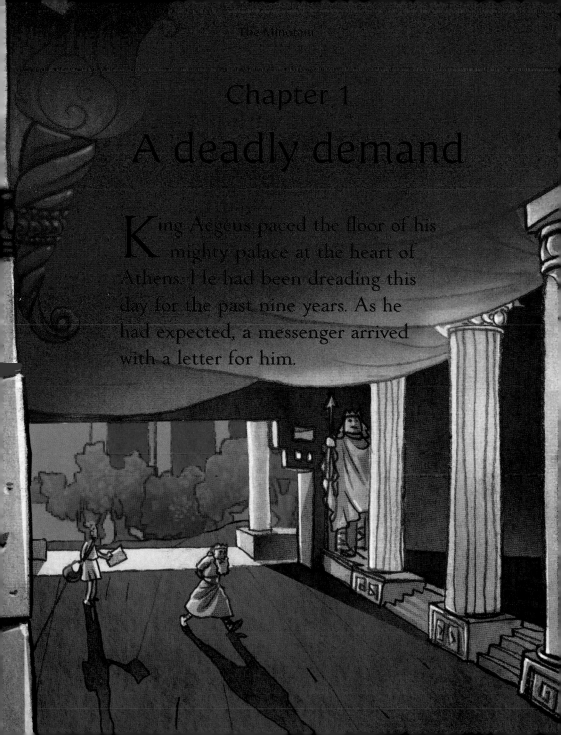

"Oh no," sighed Aegeus, as he read the contents of the letter. "Not again. What shall I do?"

"What's wrong?" asked his son, Theseus.

King Aegeus waved the letter under Theseus's nose. "Read this," he moaned. "It's from Minos, that cold-hearted king of Crete."

To: King Aegeus of Athens

Send fourteen of your people
to me by the end of the month.

signed
King Minos of Crete

P.S. I want 7 men and 7 women
P.P.S. If you don't do as I ask,
there will be trouble!

"I don't understand," said Theseus.

"Minos's son died here in Athens," explained Aegeus. "As revenge, every nine years, he demands fourteen of our people."

"What for?" asked Theseus.

"He sends them into a giant maze called the Labyrinth," replied Aegeus.

"Sounds fun," said Theseus.

"Fun?" spluttered his father. "At the heart of the Labyrinth lies a Minotaur."

"It's a terrible creature," Aegeus added. "It's half man, half bull... and it eats people!"

Chapter 2

Theseus has a plan

"What am I to do?" moaned Aegeus.
"I have an idea," said Theseus with a grin.
"I'll be one of the seven men."

"Are you insane?" cried his father. He knew Theseus was brave, but this was madness. "The Minotaur will eat you alive," he wailed.

"Don't worry, Dad," smiled Theseus. "I'm the best sword fighter in the whole of Athens."

Aegeus sighed. "Even if you kill the monster, no one has ever escaped from the Labyrinth. They say it's impossible to find your way out."

"There's always a way," said Theseus confidently. "I'm sure I can solve Minos's maze."

King Aegeus begged his son not to go. But it was no use. Theseus's mind was made up.

A few days later, Theseus
boarded a ship with the others.
Aegeus was still very worried.

"If Theseus survives," he said to the sailors,
"fly white sails on the ship when you return."

Chapter 3

Island of danger

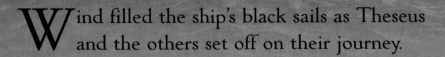

Wind filled the ship's black sails as Theseus and the others set off on their journey.

When they finally arrived at Crete, Minos's armed soldiers were waiting on the shore to escort them to the palace.

Theseus and the others were taken to the throne room and thrown at the king's feet.

"Welcome!" roared King Minos. "Enjoy your last meal. At dawn you enter the Labyrinth."

Guards took the prisoners away and locked them in a dark, dank dungeon.

As night fell, Theseus prepared himself for what was to come. After a while, Ariadne, the king's daughter, appeared with food for the prisoners.

As soon as she saw Theseus, Ariadne fell madly in love. She couldn't believe how handsome he was.

The pair talked for hours. "I can't let you spend the rest of your life in the Labyrinth," sighed Ariadne.

"Then help me to kill the Minotaur and escape," said Theseus. He needed an accomplice and Ariadne was in a perfect position to help.

Ariadne thought for a moment. "Very well," she said. "If you promise to marry me."

"Er, all right," Theseus croaked, nervously. He didn't plan to get married for a long time, if ever. But he had to agree with Ariadne for now.

Ariadne was overjoyed. "Take this ball of magic string," she said, breathlessly. "Tie it to the entrance of the Labyrinth as you go in."

"Then what?" asked Theseus.
"You'll see," smiled Ariadne.

Chapter 4

Into the Labyrinth

At dawn, the prisoners were marched to the entrance of the Labyrinth. As well as the string, Ariadne had given Theseus a sword. He did his best to hide them both under his cloak.

The doors were opened and the prisoners marched inside. When the guards weren't looking, Theseus tied one end of his string by the door.

The guards went back outside, slamming the doors behind them. "I just hope Ariadne wasn't trying to trick me," thought Theseus.

At that instant, the ball
of string jumped from
his hand.

Theseus couldn't believe his eyes. The string
rolled along the ground by itself and hurtled into
the maze. "After it!" ordered Theseus.

"What's going on?" wondered the others.
"Trust me!" said Theseus. "Just follow the string."
He had a good idea where it might lead.

The magical twine wound this way and that.
Soon they were deep, deep inside the Labyrinth.

The string came to a sudden halt in a large, stinking cavern.

"Now what?" asked one of the women.

As if in answer, a terrifying, inhuman roar echoed all around them.

"Now we face the Minotaur," cried Theseus.

Chapter 5

The Minotaur

The others trembled with fear.

"Don't worry," said Theseus, pulling out his sword with a flourish. "I'll tackle the brute. Just stand well back."

The ground shook. Heavy footsteps came nearer... and nearer. Finally, the mighty Minotaur stormed into the cave.

Raaaggghh!

It was the scariest creature Theseus had ever seen. The other prisoners gasped and screamed in terror.

Theseus gripped his sword tightly and prepared himself for the fight of his life.

The Minotaur gave a loud snort. Clouds of smelly breath shot from its nostrils.

Its eyes burned red like two hot coals. Menacingly, it stared at Theseus.

Then, with an ear-splitting roar, it charged. The young prince swung his sword at the terrifying monster.

82

Theseus felt his weapon slice the creature's skin. The Minotaur was wounded, but it didn't give up. It chased Theseus around the cave.

"Come on, Theseus!" shouted the others, as they cowered in the shadows. "Don't let it get us."

Time after time, the monster dodged Theseus's blows. Soon the young prince was struggling for breath. How much longer could he go on?

Suddenly he tripped, and looked up to see the Minotaur looming over him. The hungry creature reached out its massive hands to grab him.

This was Theseus's last chance. If he didn't kill the Minotaur now, it would kill him. With one last thrust, Theseus picked up his sword and plunged it into the monster's chest.

The Minotaur gave a blood-chilling cry. It reeled backwards, clawing at the air. Then, with a final moan, it thudded to the ground in a haze of dust.

"Well done, Theseus!" cried the others, leaping out from the shadows. "You've saved us all."

"It's not over yet," panted Theseus. "Remember we still have to find a way out of this place."

Chapter 6

Escape

Theseus noticed the magic string lying on the ground. "Of course," he said. "This will help us get back to the entrance." Picking up the ball, he followed the twine out of the cavern.

"Come on, everyone, follow me!" Theseus shouted. The prisoners cautiously trailed after him. They weaved in and out of the maze of tunnels, guided all the while by the magic thread.

At last, they reached the doors through which they had entered.

The prisoners crept up behind the guards outside. At a signal from Theseus, they grabbed the two men and tied them up with the string.

At the dock, Theseus found Ariadne waiting
patiently for him. He climbed aboard his ship.

"Don't forget your promise to marry me,"
said Ariadne, rushing after him.

"Promise?" said Theseus vaguely. "Oh, er, yes.
Absolutely. You'd better come with us."

Chapter 7

The broken promise

On the voyage home, the ship stopped at the tranquil island of Naxos.

"We'll spend the night here," announced Theseus.

But Theseus couldn't sleep. He didn't want to
marry King Minos's daughter. She'd bossed him
around ever since they left Crete.

So while Ariadne was asleep, he woke the others
and ordered them back to the ship. Quietly, they
sailed away into the night.

When Ariadne woke the next morning, she was heartbroken. She looked skywards and cried to the gods for revenge. "Make that cheat Theseus pay for deserting me!" she begged in frustration.

A magical glow filled the air, and a god named Dionysus appeared. Ariadne told him her tale.

Dionysus felt sorry for the abandoned princess. "I will punish Theseus for breaking his promise to you," he declared, dramatically raising his arms.

The god cast a spell across the sea.
"Forget, sailors!" he boomed.
"Forget, forget, forget!"

Chapter 8

A black day

By now, Theseus was nearly home. "I can't wait to be back in Athens," he told one of the sailors. "My father will be so proud of me."

"Um, yes," said the man, looking up at the black sails. His thoughts were elsewhere.

"What's the matter?" asked Theseus.

"It's funny, but I'm sure I was supposed to do something," replied the sailor. "But for the life of me, I can't remember what it was."

"That's a coincidence," said another sailor. "I had the same, strange feeling."

"And me," cried a third.

"Oh well," said Theseus, "I'm sure it can't have been anything important."

Up on the cliffs, King Aegeus looked out to sea. "My son's ship has returned at last," he sighed.

But then he saw something that broke his heart. "Oh no, black sails!" he sobbed. "My brave son Theseus must be dead."

Aegeus was grief stricken. Without thinking, he plunged into the sea and sank to his doom.

When Theseus landed, he heard the dreadful news about his father and broke down in tears.

Theseus had succeeded in his mission. He had beaten the mighty Minotaur and escaped from the perilous Labyrinth...

...but his poor father would never know.

Bellerophon and Pegasus

Retold by
Susanna Davidson

Illustrated by
Simona Bursi

Contents

Chapter 1

An impossible task

The King of Lycia had a problem. A young prince, named Bellerophon, had come to stay. For days they had been getting to know each other – laughing, riding and talking. But soon, he was going to have to kill him.

Bellerophon had arrived with a letter from the king's son-in-law. The king put it aside at first, forgetting to open it. When he finally read it, he gasped aloud...

When he stayed with us, Bellerophon was very rude to my wife – your daughter. I want you to kill him.

King Proetus

The king worried for days. "I can't do it," he thought. "I like the prince. He seems so charming, so friendly. Besides, I can't kill a guest."

"But nor can I refuse King Proetus..."

At last, the king knew what to do. He would set Bellerophon an impossible task.

"There's a terrible creature in my kingdom," the king said, over supper that night. "It's called the Chimera. I want you to kill it."

Bellerophon gulped. He couldn't say no to the king. But the Chimera breathed fire and had the head of a lion...

...the body of a goat...

...and a snake for a tail.

"The Chimera's been killing my people and ruining their land. I need your help," the king went on. Bellerophon turned pale. He knew it was deadly.

Many brave men had tried to kill the Chimera before. All of them had failed. But he had no choice.

"I accept the challenge," said Bellerophon.
He set out the next day, certain it would be
his last.

"How will I ever kill the Chimera?" he wondered
aloud. "Is it even possible?"

As he spoke, a wizened old man appeared on the road ahead. Bellerophon jumped.

"Oh it's possible," said the man. "But you can't do it alone. You'll need to listen carefully."

Bellerophon was filled with sudden hope. "This must be a wise man," he thought. "Perhaps, with his help, I can defeat the Chimera after all..."

"The monster breathes fire from its mouth," the old man went on. "But tackle it from behind, and its tail will spit deadly venom."

"You'll never get close enough to kill it
— unless you can approach it by air."
"By air?" wondered Bellerophon.

"You need Pegasus," the old man declared. "He's
a flying horse with feathery white wings who
swoops through the air like a bird...

114

...But no one has ever ridden him before."
"How do I catch him?" asked Bellerophon.

"You'll only catch him with the help of the gods,"
the man replied. "Pegasus cannot be easily tamed."

115

"See the temple on the hill?" he asked. "Sleep there tonight and help will come to you."

"Thank you!" said Bellerophon, glancing at the temple. When he turned back, the old man had gone.

Chapter 2
The golden bridle

Stars danced in the midnight sky. The moon shone brightly. Bellerophon lay on the smooth stone floor and closed his eyes. Sleep came quickly, stealing over him with a coverlet of dreams.

He saw a goddess standing before him, tall and powerful, dressed in a blaze of gold.

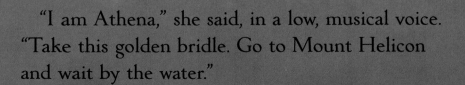

"I am Athena," she said, in a low, musical voice. "Take this golden bridle. Go to Mount Helicon and wait by the water."

"When the winged horse comes to drink, place this bridle over his head."

"If you can catch him, he will be yours to ride. Now, sleep until morning comes," she added, gently brushing his eyelids.

119

The goddess had gone when Bellerophon awoke.
But to his amazement the golden bridle was still
there, glittering in his hands.

"Pegasus could be mine!" gasped Bellerophon. And he set out for Mount Helicon.

Chapter 3

Pegasus

Bellerophon crouched by a bubbling stream, his eyes fixed on a pearl-white horse. The horse bent his head to drink, his golden hooves sparkling in the morning sun.

Bellerophon crept forward. His bare feet padded silently across the soft grass, his heart was in his mouth. He knew this was his only chance...

Quick as a flash, Bellerophon slipped the bridle over the horse's head. Pegasus neighed and struggled, bucking and rearing.

He beat the air with his powerful wings, desperate to escape.

Bellerophon clung tight to the reins, even as he felt himself dragged from the ground. He whispered words of calm to Pegasus.

The horse gave a whinny. He bowed his head and dropped to the ground.

"You're mine now," said Bellerophon, stroking his silky soft neck. "Let's ride together."

His heart beating, he climbed onto Pegasus's back. The horse grew calmer still.

"It must be a magic bridle," realized Bellerophon.

"And now," he thought, "I'm going to fly..."
"Take to the skies!" he commanded.

Pegasus leaped into the air and
they soared higher and higher, over
treetops and hills...

...over mountains, through
clouds and up into the
airy blue.

Bellerophon guided Pegasus to the rocky land where the monstrous Chimera lived. Even from the sky, he could see it clearly, huge and deadly.

As they swooped down to take a closer look, the beast began belching out smoke and fire. Its lion's mouth roared and growled, its tail writhed and hissed. Bellerophon clung tightly to the golden reins.

On furiously beating wings, Pegasus hovered above the Chimera. Bellerophon didn't want the horse to tire. He knew it was now or never. Swallowing his fear, he raised his arm and called out, "Charge!"

Chapter 4

The Chimera

Pegasus dived down to earth, a streak of white lightning in the morning sky. The wind whipped through Bellerophon's hair as they flew.

He pulled out his bow and arrow, aimed at the lion's head... and fired.

The Chimera roared in anger. It leaped out of the way and shot out a blast of flames.

Bellerophon pulled Pegasus back to the safety of the skies and aimed his arrow again. This time it hit home, piercing the Chimera's side.

Now the creature was angrier than ever. Its snake's head spat venom at Bellerophon. He twisted away, just in time. Then he urged Pegasus to spin around, swooping down at the Chimera with his spear at the ready.

The Chimera bared his teeth, his head thrown back. He started to rear up, ready to swipe at the horse, desperate to attack. Pegasus bravely flew on, heading straight for him.

As the Chimera opened its mouth to breathe fire, Bellerophon plunged his spear deep into the monster's throat.

The spear melted in the fiery heat. The Chimera struggled, choked and gasped as the molten metal flooded its throat...

VICTORY!

It rose up in
one last effort,
then slumped
to the ground,
dead at last.

Chapter 5

Flying to the gods

"I have done the impossible," Bellerophon told the king proudly. "I tamed Pegasus and together we killed the Chimera, just as you asked."

The king was amazed.

"You must have had the gods on your side," he said. "You have proved yourself a brave man."

"Now come with me," the king went on. "My people will want to thank you."

And they did. Everyone rushed to meet him.

"You're a hero," they shouted from the streets.
"You killed the Chimera. You're like a god!"
As word spread, Bellerophon became famous
across the land.

"Maybe I am a god," thought Bellerophon, swelling with pride. "After all, I have a horse that can fly... I can kill monsters where other men fail..."

Bellerophon decided it was time to visit the gods.
He swung himself onto Pegasus and they flew to
Mount Olympus, the highest mountain of all.

143

Zeus, King of the Gods, saw Bellerophon coming. "How dare he?" he thundered. "No human should ever come to the land of the gods."

He sent down an insect to sting Pegasus under his tail. Pegasus bucked and reared.

Bellerophon desperately tried to cling on, but his fingers slipped through Pegasus's silky mane and he tumbled through the sky.

Zeus watched him fall. Then he reached out with his great fist, caught Pegasus by the bridle and rode him home to Mount Olympus.

From that day, Pegasus lived with the
gods, carrying thunderbolts for Zeus.

Bellerophon crashed back to earth, his legs crumpling beneath him. He called out, but no one came to help.

He was left to wander alone, for the rest of his days, all his former glory gone. No one would go near him now his arrogance had angered the gods.

As a reward for his faithful service, Zeus placed Pegasus among the stars when he died.

You can still see
him there today.

The Twelve Tasks of Heracles

Retold by
Alex Frith

Illustrated by
Linda Cavallini

Contents

Heracles is often known by the name Hercules.
This name was used by the Romans who
worshipped him as a god. But the Greeks,
who first told his story, called him Heracles.

Chapter 1
"What have I done?"

Heracles was strong, brave and cheerful. Even though he was still a young man, he had already earned a reputation as a hero, and had married a princess. But today, he sat with his head in his hands, sobbing.

"What have I done?" he groaned. "My wife and children are dead, and it's all my fault!"

The night before, Heracles had eaten a great feast. But he didn't know that the goddess Hera had poisoned his wine. The poison drove Heracles crazy, and he began to see things.

He saw his family turn into wild animals, and was terrified that they were going to eat him. Frantically, he lashed out. He was so strong, he killed them all.

Hera was the wife of Zeus, the king of the gods, but Zeus was not a good husband. All too often, he spent time with other women. He even had children with them.

Heracles was one of these children. Zeus adored him – but Hera hated him. She wanted to make Heracles suffer, so she could get revenge on her cheating husband.

By the next day, Heracles had finally stopped sobbing. But he was still distraught, so he went to a temple to pray to his father, Zeus.

"Heracles, I am ashamed of you!" bellowed Zeus. "But I will forgive you, if you can prove your strength, courage and determination."

"Go to King Eurystheus in Tiryns. He will set you ten tasks. You must complete them all."

Eurystheus was a loyal servant of Hera. Heracles knew the tasks wouldn't be easy. But if there was any chance he could make up for the terrible thing he had done, he was going to take it.

157

Chapter 2

Wild beasts

"Your first task is to kill the Nemean lion," said King Eurystheus, "and no cheating! You must bring back its skin as proof, so I'll know you've killed the real lion."

Heracles picked up his bow and some arrows, his sword and his wooden club. Then, he set off for the town of Nemea to find the lion.

When he arrived, the Nemeans laughed at him. "You'll never kill the lion," they scoffed. "It has such a tough skin that no weapon can pierce it."

Sure enough, when Heracles fired an arrow at the lion, it bounced off. He hit it with his sword, but the blade bent. The lion snarled and opened its mouth wide, baring huge fangs.

BONK!

Heracles smashed his wooden club on the lion's head. The lion was stunned. Heracles quickly grabbed the lion's neck in his mighty arms.

He squeezed tighter... and tighter... until the lion was dead. But the lion's skin was far too tough to be cut off with his sword. Instead, he used the lion's own sharp claws.

Heracles tied the skin around his neck. The first task was complete.

"I can see that you're strong enough to kill a simple lion," said King Eurystheus. "But can you kill the terrifying hydra of Lerna?"

The hydra was a creature with many long, snake-like heads. Each one spat poisonous venom. Many brave men had tried to kill it, but most died.

Heracles was very sure of himself. He even asked his nephew Iolaus to come along and watch this task.

Iolaus drove a fine chariot with two swift horses. Heracles stood beside him, and the two headed for Lerna and the cave where the hydra lived.

Heracles set fire to some branches just in front of the cave. Thick smoke billowed into the cave mouth. The hydra poked a head out to see what was happening.

Heracles was ready for it. With one swipe of his sword, he slashed off the hydra's head. "This is easy!" he shouted to Iolaus.

But then something astonishing happened. Two new heads grew out of the wound in the hydra's neck and they spat dark venom at Heracles.

"What can I do?" shouted Heracles, as he dodged the venom. "I'll never be able to kill the hydra if it keeps growing new heads."

Iolaus had an idea. He grabbed one of the burning branches. "Quick, uncle," he called. "Cut off another head."

As soon as the head came off, Iolaus set fire to the stump. No new heads could grow.

Together, Heracles and Iolaus cut off and burned every one of the hydra's heads.

Before heading home, Heracles took a few arrows and dipped them in the hydra's venom.

"You never know when poison arrows might be useful!" he said.

Chapter 3
Run, Heracles, run

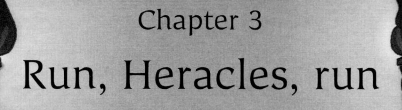

"That last task doesn't count!" shouted
Eurystheus. "Iolaus helped you, and that's
cheating. You'll have to do another task." But
secretly, Eurystheus was impressed.

"You've proved you're strong and brave, but are
you quick enough to catch the Erymanthian boar?"

The boar was a large, unfriendly creature that lived at the bottom of Mount Erymanthus. It caused endless trouble for the local farmers.

Heracles chased the boar all the way up the mountain, but he couldn't catch it. Whenever he got close, the boar jumped just out of reach.

After an entire day of chasing, Heracles was exhausted – but he didn't give up.

At last, the boar jumped to the very top of the mountain. It landed in a patch of snow and slipped.

Heracles didn't waste a second. He pounced on the boar, and quickly tied it up. He dragged it back to Tiryns, with a proud grin on his face.

170

"Take it away!" screamed King Eurystheus. Terrified, he jumped into a giant pot to hide from the boar. Gingerly lifting the lid, he peered out to give Heracles his next task.

"Boars are foolish creatures. Your next task will be much tougher. Catch the Ceryneian deer – the fastest animal on earth!"

Heracles chased the deer from one end of the world to the other, but he couldn't catch it. The deer was so fast, it even outran Heracles's arrows.

Finally, after a year of running, the deer stopped at a lake for a drink.

Heracles hid in a bush. Very quietly, he fired an arrow. Just then, a loud voice boomed out of the trees...

"How dare you shoot my deer?" said the voice. Heracles turned to see Artemis, the goddess of wild animals, towering over him.

Heracles knelt down and begged for mercy. Artemis took pity on him, and gave him the deer.

Chapter 4

Dirty work

"That task took you a whole year!" laughed King Eurystheus. "For your next task, go and clean out the stables of King Augeas – in a single day."

King Augeas was delighted to see Heracles. "My stables are the filthiest in the land," he said. "Are you really going to clean them up in one day?"

Heracles was very confident. "I bet you I can do it," he boasted.

"If you can manage it, I'll give you a hundred of my cows," promised Augeas.

Inside the stables, piles of mucky manure towered high, and they smelled disgusting. No one had cleaned the place in years. But Heracles set to work with a shovel, smiling.

After a hour, he stopped smiling. There was simply too much muck.

Heracles rested on the shovel and wondered what he could do. He looked up, and through a window in the stables, he saw a river.

The river gave him an idea. Using the shovel, he knocked a big hole in the wall. Then he flung open the stable doors.

He began to dig a long ditch. By noon, it reached from the back of the stables all the way to the river.

Next, he found a massive boulder, and dropped it into the river. The water hit the boulder and ran off into the ditch. Soon, great floods of water swept through the stables, washing out all the muck in an instant.

Augeas gasped in amazement.

Once again, Heracles went back to Tiryns triumphant. A whole herd of cows came with him.

For a change, King Eurystheus was looking happy. "You may have cleaned the stables," he said, "but it's not right to get paid for doing a task, even in cows. That task doesn't count!"

Heracles didn't mind. He was feeling stronger and more heroic with each task. He was ready for the next challenge.

Chapter 5

Dangerous animals

Eurystheus quickly thought up three more tasks for Heracles. First, he sent him to shoot down a flock of deadly birds that attacked anyone who wandered into the forest of Stymphalia.

The birds scratched at Heracles with their claws, and feathers made of sharp bronze. But he was protected by the skin of the Nemean lion. Heracles scared the birds away from the treetops by shaking a thunderous rattle, and killed them all with his bow and arrows.

Then, Heracles had to visit the island of Crete to tame a fire-breathing bull. Throwing a lasso, he snagged its neck and held on tight. Heracles leaped up into the air, and landed with a thump on the bull's back.

After that trick, he had to capture five fearsome, man-eating mares that belonged to Diomedes, a wicked king who lived in Thrace.

Diomedes tried to trick Heracles into entering the stables. But at the last minute, Heracles grabbed a rope, bound the king, and trapped him inside with the hungry mares.

Heracles listened outside the stable door. He heard the mares chomping and chewing, and then snoring as they fell asleep. Heracles tied them up and dragged them to Tiryns.

Hera had been watching Heracles complete his tasks. She was not at all happy, and came down from Olympus to shout at Eurystheus.

"Heracles must not finish all his tasks," said Hera. "I don't want him to become a hero."

"But he's so brave and strong, and he's quite clever, too," replied Eurystheus. "I can't think of any harder tasks to set him."

"Hmm," said Hera. "Well, he's hunted all sorts of animals, killed a few monsters and outwitted a man, but there's one kind of foe he hasn't faced yet. Let's see how well he does against a woman!"

185

Chapter 6

Heracles and the women

Eurystheus summoned Heracles to his court. "For your ninth task, go to the island of the Amazons, where only women are allowed, and steal the belt worn by Hippolyta, their queen."

Heracles found a rowing boat and set off. As he rowed, he tried to think of a clever way to sneak onto the island, but he had no ideas.

From the clouds above, Hera watched him, confident that he wouldn't even find the Amazons, let alone beat Queen Hippolyta in a fight.

But when Heracles arrived, he found Queen Hippolyta herself, waiting for him on the shore. She seemed pleased to see him.

"Are you the famous Heracles, who killed the lion and the hydra?" she asked.

"I am," said Heracles, with a friendly smile.

"Most men are weak, but you must be strong. We want to hear all about your tasks. Come onto our island and eat dinner with us."

At dinner, Heracles soon charmed Hippolyta
with his tales of bravery, strength and cunning.
Then he told the story of how he killed his family.

Hippolyta was moved to tears, and she gave him
her belt so he could complete his latest task.

This made one of the dinner guests furious. It was Hera, who had disguised herself as an Amazon warrior. She couldn't bear to see Heracles win.

Hera whispered into the ear of the woman next to her. "See how close he is to our queen. He doesn't want her belt — he wants to kidnap her!"

Very quickly, the lie spread around the room. Heracles looked up from his food to see a crowd of angry faces, staring at him.

Heracles grabbed the belt, and charged out of the room. Fighting his way to the beach, he managed to jump back into his boat – just in time.

Chapter 7
Far-off lands

Heracles was exhausted. He had hoped to rest before his tenth task began, but Eurystheus didn't want to wait.

"Go to the island where the monster Geryon lives," he said. "And bring me his cows."

192

Wearily, Heracles got back into his boat. It was a blazing hot day and Heracles shouted angrily at Helios, the god of the sun. "Do you have to make this task harder?" he yelled, firing an arrow at him.

Helios caught the arrow.
He felt sorry for Heracles.
"Take my golden boat," he said.
"It's strong enough to carry the sun, and it will
help you cross the ocean."

Heracles watched as a boat shaped like a lotus
plant slowly dropped from the sky.

Even in Helios's boat, it took Heracles months to reach Geryon's island. By the time he arrived, he was rested and ready to fight.

His first challenge was Geryon's two-headed dog. Heracles struck the beast with his wooden club and the dog flew into the sea.

HOOOOOWL!

With the same club, he knocked Geryon's servant into the ground.

Then, a huge shadow fell over Heracles. He looked up and saw Geryon for the first time. Heracles couldn't believe his eyes.

Geryon had three ugly heads and six bulging arms on one body. It was as if three ogres had fused into one gigantic, hideous monster...

196

Geryon roared at
Heracles with his three
mouths, and drew three
massive swords.

Heracles ran
away and hid,
wondering
how he could
defeat such a
dangerous foe.

The answer came to him in a flash. He reached behind his back and pulled out a special arrow.

It was one of the arrows he had dipped into the hydra's venom.

Heracles fired a single shot. He watched as the arrow pierced Geryon through one neck, then another, then a third. The monster was dead.

But the task wasn't over. Heracles had to make the long journey back to Tiryns across a stormy sea. It was over a year before Heracles arrived back in Tiryns with all Geryon's cows...

...only to find Hera waiting for him. She was disguised as a mosquito, and she stung the cows so hard, they panicked and ran away.

It took Heracles another year to round them all up again, and present them to King Eurystheus.

Long ago, Prometheus had told humans the secret of making fire. Zeus had punished him by chaining him to a mountain and sending a vulture to attack him.

Heracles found Prometheus, and used his last poison arrow to shoot the vulture. He cut off the Titan's chains – and Prometheus was happy to help.

"I'm sorry," he said, "but I don't know where the garden is. Perhaps my brother, Atlas, does."

Everyone knew where to find Atlas. He was a Titan who lived at the top of the tallest mountain on earth, holding up the sky.

Heracles made the long climb to find him.

"Oh, I know where the garden of the gods is," said Atlas. "But I can't tell you."

"I'll make you a deal," said Heracles.

"If you go to the garden yourself, and fetch me an apple, I'll stay here and hold up the sky for you."

Atlas agreed. He was desperate to stand up straight and stretch his aching muscles. He gently lowered the sky onto Heracles's waiting arms.

Heracles heaved and groaned under the weight of the sky. He couldn't believe how heavy it was. But he didn't dare drop it.

What would he do if Atlas didn't come back?

But before long, Atlas returned with an apple. "Heracles," he said, "you're doing such a good job I think you should stay. Just for a year or so."

Heracles thought fast. "Of course," he said. "But the sky keeps slipping on my hands. Would you show me the best way to hold it?"

As soon as Atlas took hold of the sky, Heracles grabbed the apple and ran down the mountain. Atlas howled with rage, cursing the mischievous hero.

Chapter 8
The final task

Eurystheus was flabbergasted. Not only was Heracles strong enough to hold up the sky, he was bold enough to play a trick on a Titan.

But even Heracles couldn't go to the underworld and back... could he?

For the final task, Eurystheus sent Heracles down into Hades, the land of the dead – a place where no living man was allowed to enter.

To prove he'd been, Heracles had to bring back Cerberus, a three-headed guard dog who kept the dead from leaving.

First, Heracles had to cross the murky river Styx, but Charon, the ferryman, wouldn't take him. "I ferry the dead, not the living," he insisted.

"I am Heracles, slayer of beasts and men," boasted Heracles. "I go where I choose. Now take me across into Hades!"

Charon was so scared that he didn't argue.

No sooner had Heracles jumped out of the boat on the other side, than a spooky figure appeared in front of him. It was Persephone, the queen of Hades.

"You must turn back," she said.

"I've only come for Cerberus," Heracles replied with a grin. "I won't stay."

"If you can defeat Cerberus with your bare hands, I will let you borrow him," said Persephone.

It was the fight of Heracles's life...

...but he won.

"Well done, Heracles," said King Eurystheus. "You have proved that you are a mighty hero, the strongest, bravest man on earth!"

"Now go out into the world," bellowed Zeus. "You are forgiven."

A hero's life

Even when he was a tiny baby, Hera plotted to kill Heracles. She dropped a snake into his crib one night...

Heracles strangled it with his bare hands.

Not all the gods hated Heracles. Athena and Apollo gave him magical weapons for protection.

Before he began his twelve tasks, Heracles used these weapons to kill giants and sea monsters.

It took him ten years to complete all the tasks. Afterwards, he went on a long adventure with his friends Jason and the Argonauts.

Legend says that when Heracles died, he became a god.

Perseus and the Gorgon

Retold by
Lesley Sims

Illustrated by
Simona Bursi

Contents

Chapter 1

The sea monster

Long ago and deep beneath the sea, there lived a monster. This monster was ten times bigger than any whale. Its mouth was as wide as a cave, and its teeth were sharper than spears.

For years, the monster prowled the deep sea near Ancient Greece. Feeding on sharks and giant squid, it was kept firmly under control by Poseidon, God of the Seas.
But lately...

...the monster had been eating men.

Bursting from the depths, it smashed through ships, scattering fishermen into the water. Then it opened its cavernous mouth and gobbled them up with one snap of its jaws.

Villagers living near the sea were terrified of the monster, which they had named Cetus. Not knowing what else to do, they marched in a group to the royal palace, demanding to see the king.

"Cetus is murdering our fishermen!" they yelled to him. "Send your guards to kill it. You must destroy the monster!"

King Cepheus came out onto his balcony and gazed down at the angry villagers with a troubled frown. He had no idea where to start in order to save his people and his kingdom.

He went back to his throne, deep in thought. Cetus was a menace, and it was all his wife's fault. She had boasted that their daughter, Andromeda, was more beautiful than the mermaids who served Poseidon — so Poseidon had let the monster go wild.

In desperation, King Cepheus consulted a priest. The priest's advice appalled him.

"There is only one way to pacify Poseidon. You must offer your only daughter to the monster as a sacrifice."

The king and queen were grief-stricken and their young daughter, Andromeda, was petrified.

None of them knew that help was on the way — and from a surprising young man.

Chapter 2

Perseus

The young man in question was currently in trouble and hiding from royal guards. His name was Perseus and the local king, Polydectes, wanted to marry Perseus's mother. Unfortunately, she didn't want to marry the king.

Perseus had heard the king's guards were on their way and had hurried his mother from their home. As they cowered beside the back wall, they heard the tramp of the guards approaching and then a fist hammering on their front door.

"Come out!" shouted a voice. "We know you're in there."

Perseus saw his mother tremble and gave her a tight hug. "Don't worry," he reassured her. "If we're quick, we can hide in the forest. They'll have to go back to Polydectes without us."

Tugging her hand, he raced down the
street. But the king seemed to have sent his
entire army. There were guards everywhere.
"Over there!" one of them yelled. "After them!"
Across the street, the village priest called to
Perseus. "This way! I'll hide you!"

Perseus didn't hear.

He pulled his mother onto
another street and ducked down an
alley. It was a dead end.

They turned to run back and found
guards now blocking the end of the alley.
The guards stomped menacingly closer.

Perseus stepped in front of his mother. "Don't come any nearer," he warned the guards.

But they kept coming. "It's just your mother we want," growled one.

Perseus hurled himself at them, hoping to barge them over, so his mother could escape. But the guards were too strong. A fist crashed against his head, and he fell to the ground.

"Tell the king I'll do anything he wants if he leaves my mother alone," Perseus cried. "I'll even bring him the head of Medusa herself."

The guards laughed in disbelief.

Medusa was a Gorgon, a monster so ugly that just one glance at her face turned men to stone.

"Ha! We'll tell him," said the guards, as they dragged his mother away.

Perseus desperately tried to lift himself up, but all the breath had been knocked out of him. "I'll fetch Medusa's head," he promised his mother, "and I'll use it to turn King Polydectes to stone."

Then pain overwhelmed him and his eyes fluttered shut.

Chapter 3
A helpful priest

Perseus woke to find himself lying on a bed in a gloomy house. Daylight shone through cracks in the wooden walls, dazzling his bleary eyes.

"Ah good, you're awake," said a voice.

"Huh?" said Perseus, struggling to see.

The village priest was watching him.

"Aagh..." Perseus started to sit up and moaned, as pain shot through his head. "Where am I? What happened?"

"I saw you trying to save your mother from the king's guards," said the priest. "And I heard what you said about Medusa. But you were in no state to fight anything, so I brought you to my house to recover."

"Now," he went on, "there are things you need to know. First, your father…"

"Oh, I don't know who he is," Perseus interrupted, "I've never met him."

"I'm not surprised," the priest replied. "It's Zeus, King of the Gods."

"What?" cried Perseus, astounded.

"My father is Zeus?" he repeated. "But that means I'm half a god! King Polydectes won't be able to stop me. I must go to the palace and rescue my mother at once." And he stood up from the bed.

At once, the priest sprang in front of him, blocking the door.

"Don't be a fool," he said. "You wouldn't get anywhere near your mother. The palace has hundreds of guards. There's no way you can defeat them on your own, whoever your father was."

"No," he went on, "you must do as you promised your mother. Find and kill the Gorgon Medusa, then come back and turn her head on the king."

Now Perseus looked doubtful. "Even if I am Zeus's son," he said, "can I really defeat Medusa? Some of the country's bravest warriors have tried and all of them failed."

"The gods will send gifts to help," said the priest. As he spoke, a razor-sharp sword and shimmering shield appeared. "The sword will cut anything," he explained. "And you can look at Medusa safely in the shield. Her reflection has no power."

He went to a cupboard, took out a leather bag and handed it to Perseus. "For the Gorgon's head," he said grimly. "Now, go to the forest and find the three witches. Only they know where Medusa lives."

Chapter 4

Witches of the forest

Perseus headed for the forest as quickly as he could. The shield was heavy, and the sword swung awkwardly from his belt, catching him on the legs as he ran, but he knew he would need both to stand any chance of defeating Medusa. First, though, he had to find the witches.

Reaching the forest, Perseus darted between the trees, slowing slightly as the light grew dim. The wind whispered in the treetops and, as he went further in, only a few lonely shafts of sunlight pierced their tangled branches. But there was another light up ahead – firelight.

Three wrinkled old crones sat around a bubbling cauldron, which was giving off foul-smelling fumes. Perseus tried not to choke as he crept closer – and then shuddered when he saw that the witches had no eyes, only empty sockets, dark and dead inside.

One of the witches sprang up. "Who's there?" she shrieked. "Who dares to enter our forest?"

Rummaging in her pocket, she pulled out a slippery eyeball. She slotted it into her eye socket and glared at Perseus across the fire.

"Oooh," she said. "It's a warrior. A fine, strong warrior with a heavy sword and shield, looking straight at us with his clear, brown eyes."

"Let me see!" snapped another of the witches. She shuffled around the cauldron to the first witch, plucked the eyeball from her face and shoved it into her own.

She blinked a couple of times and smiled. "Oooh," she cooed. "He does have lovely eyes."

"Give me that!" demanded the third witch, snatching the eyeball.

As she peered at Perseus, her gummy mouth spread into a nasty grin. "Oooh," she gurgled. "He has lovely, shiny eyes."

"Enough talk about eyes!" said Perseus.
"I need to find the Gorgon Medusa."

The witches began to cackle. "Medusa?"
they shrieked. "He seeks Medusa! No one ever
makes it out of Medusa's cave alive, warrior."

"Cave?" said Perseus. "Which cave? Tell me!"

"Ah," said the third witch, "but there is a price for that information."

"Name it."

The witch stepped closer, grinning hideously. "We want your lovely eyes," she said, and she reached up with her claw-like hands, as if to snatch them from his face.

"Hey!" cried Perseus, leaping back.

These old hags were crazy, Perseus
thought, but he needed their help. "Very
well," he said at last, sliding out his sword.
"I will give you my eyes."

The witches scuttled closer, drooling with
excitement. "Let me see," they squabbled.
"Give me our eye!"

Fast as a flash, Perseus lashed out his
sword and knocked the stinking cauldron
onto the fire. A cloud of steam billowed
out, hissing and spitting in the witches'
shocked faces.

The three staggered back, dropping their precious eyeball on the ground.

Perseus snatched it up and placed it on his palm. "I have your eye," he said. "Now tell me where Medusa lives or I'll squash it like a bug."

The witches squirmed.

"We can't tell you," said the first.

"Medusa would hurt us," said the second.

"My hand is closing on your eye," said Perseus.

"Tell him!" the third witch screamed. "Tell him! Tell him!"

"She lives in a cave," said the first witch, sulkily.
"So you said. Which cave?" Perseus demanded.

"Beneath the Black Mountain. The Cave of the Dragon's Mouth," muttered the second witch.

Satisfied, Perseus tossed them the eyeball. Then he turned and raced from the forest.

"You'll die warrior!" the witches shrieked. "Everyone dies in Medusa's cave!"

Chapter 5

The Dragon's Mouth

Dark clouds swirled overhead as Perseus emerged from the forest. A flash of lightning streaked across the sky. Perseus was tired and cold, but he kept going until he reached a slope of dark rocks – the Black Mountain.

Jagged stalactites hung from the entrance to a cave, like the fangs of some terrible beast. This was the Cave of the Dragon's Mouth. This was where Medusa lived. Perseus's grip tightened around his sword. He tried to stop himself from trembling as he stepped inside...

Ducking his head to avoid the stalactites, he went deeper into the cave. It grew colder, and pale rays of light shining in from outside cast eerie

shadows. In the gloom, strange shapes loomed up at him. They seemed to be statues of men, perfectly carved from the rock.

Perseus looked more closely. No, he realized with a horrified shiver... They *were* men. These were the brave warriors who had tried to kill Medusa. Each one had managed to track her down, only to be turned to stone by her evil glare. Frozen faces leered at him, caught at the moment they saw her, mouths open in silent screams, and eyes wide with terror.

At the heart of the cave, something moved. Quickly, Perseus hid behind one of the stone warriors. Hisses echoed around the cave, bouncing off the walls, growing louder and louder.

Don't look, Perseus told himself. Just don't look. If he dared a single glance at Medusa, he would be turned to stone too.

As he crouched behind the unlucky stone figure, the priest's words came back to him.

...you can look at Medusa safely in the shield. Her reflection has no power.

Perseus raised his shield slowly in the direction of the hissing – and saw her at last.

He had heard stories about her, but none of them had prepared him for how monstrous the Gorgon truly was.

She had a long, worm-like body, jagged teeth, blood-red eyes and lethal-looking claws. Most grotesque of all, dozens of snakes writhed where her hair should have been, snapping, hissing and baring their vicious fangs. Suddenly, the snakes turned and stared at the exact place where Perseus was hiding.

They had seen him!

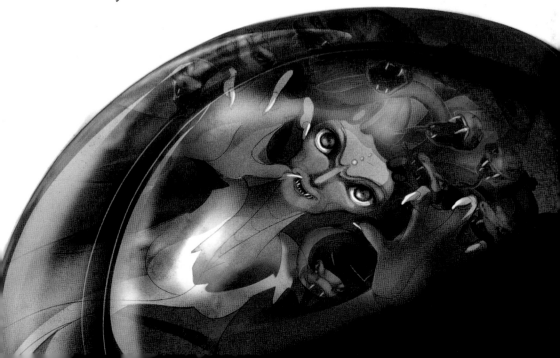

Perseus's heart raced as Medusa slithered
closer. In his shield, he saw the snakes on her
head wriggle and writhe.

"Warrior..." they hissed. "Look at usss, warrior. Look at usss and your troublesss will all be over."

No! Perseus thought again. If he looked at them, he'd be turned to stone. He had to strike fast and catch Medusa by surprise.

Gathering his courage, he burst
from his hiding place. He held his
shield up high and whirled his sword
at the Gorgon.

But Medusa was too fast
and too strong. Catching Perseus's
arm, she flung him across the cave.
Rocks tumbled from the walls, crashing
down on Perseus as he fell to the floor.

Perseus tried to scramble up, but his legs
were caught under the rocks. He couldn't
reach his sword...

...and in his shield, he saw Medusa approach.

"Look at usss warrior," the snakes hissed. "Look at ussssssssss."

Perseus stared at the hideous face in horror as it came ever closer.

The monster grasped Perseus's back, starting to roughly turn him around. Perseus tried to fight her, but she had the strength of one hundred warriors.

At once, he shut his eyes. Feeling around, he found and grabbed hold of a rock and rammed the jagged edge into Medusa's hand.

Medusa gave a piercing scream.

Perseus twisted from her grasp. Then, careful to look only at the cave ceiling, he hurled the rock at a stalactite.

With a mighty crack, the stalactite broke off. It shot down towards Medusa, slicing straight through her neck and cutting her head from her body in seconds.

Perseus dragged himself back to his shield and held it up to see what had happened. There was the severed head's reflection. To his relief, the snakes still hissed and spat. He prayed they had kept their power to turn King Polydectes to stone.

Making sure to keep his eyes firmly shut,
Perseus placed the head in his leather bag. He
ached all over, but there was no time to rest —
he had to rescue his mother. Taking a deep breath,
Perseus turned and staggered from the cave.

Chapter 6
Attack of the sea monster

The moment he left the cave, Perseus was blasted by a gale that nearly swept him from his feet. And the storm only grew stronger as he struggled back towards the coast. Icy rain lashed against his face, and fierce winds threatened to tear the bag from his hands. But he held on tight, feeling the snakes on Medusa's head wriggle inside.

He was well on his way when he saw a crowd
gathered at the top of a cliff in the distance,
staring out to the stormy sea.

Perseus was baffled. What on earth could be
going on? Then he spotted a beautiful young
woman at the bottom of the cliff, being chained
to the rock by some soldiers. She stared solemnly
ahead, patiently letting them bind her.

With one glance at her face, Perseus fell in love.

High above the woman, a man stood
surveying the scene. He looked heartbroken.
Behind him huddled a nervous crowd.

Perseus didn't know it, but this was the
day of Andromeda's sacrifice.

Perseus watched. A dark shape rose from the depths of the sea.

"Cetus!" screamed the crowd and a monster appeared through the waves.

The monster's long fangs flashed in a streak of lightning as it swam forward. It had seen Andromeda, and it was hungry.

Perseus didn't know who they were but he knew he could rescue the girl. He reached for his bag, feeling Medusa's head inside. If he could just get this terrifying creature to look at the snakes...

Charging for the edge of the cliff, he leaped
from the end.
He fell...
and fell...
landing hard on
the monster's back.

He gripped the cold, scaly body between
his legs and held on tight. Then, with a cry, he
plunged his sword into Cetus's shoulder. The
monster's roar was louder than thunder. It thrashed
and rolled, trying to shake Perseus off. But Perseus
clung on to his sword. He was waiting for the
right moment...

"Now!" he thought.

Just as the sea creature lurched forward, Perseus let go of his sword. He was flung high in the air and into the water.

Bursting to the surface, he swam frantically for the rocks. The monster came after him, its vast mouth wide open.

With the last of his strength, Perseus hauled himself onto the rocks. "Shut your eyes!" he yelled to the girl. "Don't look!"

He reached into his bag and pulled out Medusa's head. Closing his own eyes, he thrust the grisly trophy into the air.

The monster glared furiously at the hissing snakes. Its mouth opened to roar, but no sound came out. It looked down, horrified to see its body turning to stone. But still it came after Perseus. It was moving slower and slower, but it was getting closer and closer...

The girl cried out. Perseus dropped the head and put his arms around her. The monster's shadow fell over them. Its huge mouth opened... but it didn't shut. It stood as silent and still as the cliffs. It had turned entirely to stone.

With his eyes closed once again, Perseus felt for Medusa's head and put it in his bag, before returning to comfort the girl.

"You saved my life!" she said. "And I don't even know your name."

"P... Perseus," gasped Perseus, still getting his breath back.

"Then thank you, Perseus," she said. "I'm Princess Andromeda. My father, King Cepheus, is just up there on the top of the cliffs. I know he'll want to thank you too."

As Perseus helped Andromeda up the cliff, the villagers roared and cheered in delight.

King Cepheus beamed when he was introduced to Perseus. "You must come back to the palace and celebrate with us," he said, giving Perseus a friendly pat on the back.

"I would love to, sire," said Perseus, gazing at Andromeda, "but I have some unfinished business to attend to first."

"Well, come as soon as you can," said the king.

"I'll be waiting for you," Andromeda added, with a shy smile.

With one last look at Andromeda, Perseus headed off for the palace of King Polydectes.

His mother gave a cry of relief when she saw him enter the throne room.

Perseus gave her a quick smile as he strode right up to King Polydectes and withdrew the Gorgon's gruesome remains from the bag.

The king was astounded to see Perseus return with Medusa's head. But he didn't say a word. He had leaped from his throne and now stood in silence, totally still — as still and cold as a statue.

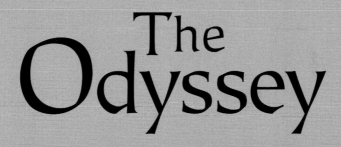

The Odyssey

Retold by
Louie Stowell

Illustrated by
Matteo Pincelli

Contents

About *The Odyssey* and Homer

The Odyssey was composed nearly 3,000 years ago in Ancient Greece, by an author named Homer, although it is based on even older tales. It is an epic poem — a poem telling a story about the adventures of mighty heroes and powerful gods.

Very little is known about Homer's life, but his works have been famous for thousands of years. He's also the author of *The Iliad*. This epic poem tells the story of the Trojan War, fought out between the Greeks and the Trojans.

Odysseus, hero of *The Odyssey*, plays a big part in *The Iliad*, too, saving the day with his cunning trick involving a large wooden horse.

Chapter 1

Calypso's prisoner

On the sandy shore of the island of Ogygia – home of the sea nymph Calypso – there sat a big strong man, sobbing his heart out. His name was Odysseus, and he was a very long way from home.

Far above him, the mighty gods of Mount Olympus were watching. Athena, Goddess of Wisdom, turned to her father, Zeus. He was king of all the gods; if anyone could help Odysseus, he could. She pointed to the tiny, ant-like human below. "Look, Father. Poor Odysseus has been stranded there for years. Will you help him to escape from Calypso's island and get home to his family?"

283

Zeus scowled, making the clouds around them crackle with lightning. "Why should I help him?" he asked. "He's just a human."

"He's not just any human, Father," said Athena. "He's a hero – and a *clever* one, at that." She smiled. "He practically won the Trojan War single-handed, and he used his brain to do it. Remember how he smuggled an army into Troy in a wooden horse? Surely he deserves some credit for that?"

Zeus chuckled: "Oh yes." But then his face darkened. "What about Poseidon, God of the Seas? He hates Odysseus and he'll be furious if I help."

"And you're King of the Gods," Athena replied. "Your word is law and all other gods must bow before you." She arched an eyebrow. "Isn't that so?"

Zeus grunted, obviously pleased. "That is true." He called to a young, handsome god nearby, "Hermes! Go and tell that pesky Calypso to let Odysseus go. The great and mighty Zeus orders it!"

Hermes saluted, scrambled into his golden winged sandals and pushed off into the empty air.

Down... down... down... until at last his golden sandals touched the soft soil of Ogygia. Hermes found himself in a beautiful forest, surrounded by lush vegetation and the delicious smell of herbs. Somewhere close by, a scented fire was burning. And then, he saw her... Calypso.

Even though Hermes was a god, who spent his days with beautiful goddesses, he was still stunned by her loveliness. "My lady," he said, with a bow.

Calypso welcomed him warmly. At least, she did until he told her why he was there...

"You want me to WHAT?" Her eyes flashed with fury. "Why should I give up Odysseus? I love him! He's lived with me for seven blissful years."

"Blissful for *you* perhaps..." said Hermes.

Calypso gave him a fiery look.

Hermes added, "Zeus commands you to let your prisoner go." He didn't need to add, *or else...*

At that, Calypso sighed. "Then I must."

Calypso padded down to the beach where Odysseus sat, staring out to sea. He looked up as he heard her footsteps.

"Zeus is forcing me to let you go," Calypso said. She fluttered her eyelashes at Odysseus. "If you really and truly want to leave, that is..."

"I want to go," said Odysseus, quickly. Perhaps a little too quickly, for Calypso began to look angry. So he added, in a tender voice, "You're incredibly beautiful, Calypso. But I want to see my wife and child and my home again. That's where I belong."

With a lovesick sigh, Calypso gave up. She helped Odysseus to build a sturdy raft and, as soon as it was ready, he sailed away without a glance in her direction.

Far above Odysseus's raft, Poseidon, God of the Seas, looked down and saw that Odysseus was free.

"Zeus let you go when I wasn't looking, did he?" he muttered. "You're not getting away that easily, little man!" Poseidon stuck his trident into the sea and stirred it up into a ferocious storm.

The winds and the rain lashed the little raft until it was smashed to pieces and Odysseus was thrown into the sea. He felt himself sinking into the freezing ocean. The deeper he sank, the colder it became. Soon, he knew no more.

When he came to, he found himself on a beach.
For a horrible moment, he thought he was back
where he'd started, on Ogygia.

Then he saw a pair of girls washing clothes
in the river close by. "This can't be Ogygia," he
thought, feeling very relieved. "I was alone with
Calypso there." He got slowly to his feet and called
out to the girls, "Hello?"

The girls gave a squeal of shock.

Odysseus bowed low. "I'm sorry I scared you. But
do you know where I might find food and shelter?"

The girls, still trembling slightly, pointed out a
palace, up a hill.

As it turned out, the king and queen who lived in the palace were the perfect hosts. Without even asking who he was, they ushered him inside, gave him fresh clothes and plenty to eat and drink.

"In return for this fine hospitality," said Odysseus, "I'll tell you all an incredible tale."

A murmur of excitement went through the court. Odysseus cleared his throat and began: "My name is Odysseus and, unfortunately for me, everything I'm about to tell you is true..."

Chapter 2

Odysseus's tale

Although you wouldn't know it to look at me, I'm a king. My kingdom is on the island of Ithaca, and I've been trying to get back there for the past seven years.

When I set sail for home, my men and I had just won a war against Troy. It took ten years and we lost many comrades. Still, twelve ships full of my men survived, and we were glad to be going home at last. At least, that was the plan...

Our journey began badly when a storm blew us off course, leaving us adrift for days. When we finally saw land, my men cheered and rushed ashore, disappearing into the thick undergrowth.

Unfortunately, the island was the land of the Lotus Eaters, where the fruit is so delicious, you never want to leave. After one taste, my men lost all interest in home. All they wanted was the fruit! I had to drag them back to the ship and lock them up before we could be on our way.

We sailed on. On the next island, we discovered a gigantic cave near the beach. Someone obviously lived there, so I said, "Men, let's wait here to see whose cave it is. Maybe he can give us supplies or, at the very least, directions?"

As it turned out, waiting was a terrible idea. The cave was the home of a Cyclops, a one-eyed giant, and his single eye wasn't at all pleased to see us.

As he arrived home with a herd of giant sheep, he roared at us, "Who are you?"

He rolled a huge stone over the entrance to trap us inside. "I am Polyphemus and this is my house! What are *you* doing here?"

I spoke up. "We're weary soldiers on our way back from a war," I said. "And, as I'm sure you know, the great god Zeus looks kindly on those who are kind to strangers." I winked at him. "So it's probably a good idea to give us food and water..."

The Cyclops burst out laughing, spraying a shower of foul-smelling spit over us all. "Zeus? Hahahahaha! I'm not afraid of him — my father is Poseidon, God of the Seas. Zeus is my uncle!"

With that, he plucked up two of my men in his meaty hands — and ate them, raw. After a swig of sheep's milk, the monster grabbed another two. Some of my men cried, "Kill him! Kill him now."

But, looking at the huge stone blocking the door, I knew I couldn't. "We'll be trapped if he dies," I whispered to Eurylochus, my right-hand man. "But I have another idea..."

297

Chapter 3

A cunning plan

I gathered a few of my men in a huddle and pointed out a branch in the corner of the cave. "Sharpen that," I told them.

Then, I turned to the Cyclops, who was eyeing up my men, deciding which poor soul to eat next.

"We have hardly any food or water, but we do have some very fine wine with us," I called. "Would you like some?"

The Cyclops beamed. "Yes! Give it to me!" He grabbed the bottle and took a swig. "What's your name, stranger?"

"My name is Nobody," I said. (This was part of my cunning plan.)

"Well, Nobody," said the Cyclops. "I shall do something nice for you, in return for the wine..."

I was about to thank him, when he went on: "Yes. I'll eat you last! Hahahahaha!"

"Oh," I said, with a gulp. "Would you like some more wine?"

Soon, just as I had hoped, the wine made him sleepy and he began to snore like a sty full of pigs.

I whispered to my men to heat the sharpened branch in the fire. When its sharp end was white-hot, we hefted it onto our shoulders and jammed it into the Cyclops's closed eye with a sizzle.

He woke with a jolt and screamed, "Owww! Help! Nobody's hurting me!"

Another giant who lived next door heard him and laughed. "If nobody's hurting you, then stop crying, you great big baby!"

Furious and whimpering in pain, the blinded Cyclops lay back down. Eventually, he cried himself to sleep.

The next morning, he rolled the stone away from the cave mouth to let his sheep out to graze in the lush green pasture beyond.

At my order, each man strapped himself quickly and quietly beneath one of the Cyclops's huge sheep. As the animals wandered out into the fields, my men escaped into the fresh, free air.

Once outside, we let the sheep go and ran back to the ship as fast as our legs would carry us. In my triumph, I couldn't resist turning back and yelling, "I tricked you, Cyclops, I'm not Nobody! I'm Odysseus!"

The Cyclops howled and began to throw rocks at us – luckily, his aim was terrible now that he couldn't see. "Father! Poseidon! God of the Seas!" he cried out. "Odysseus has blinded me. Punish him and make him suffer as I suffer!"

"Oh dear," I said to Eurylochus, as we sailed away. "Do you think telling him my real name might have been a mistake?"

Chapter 4

The bag of winds

I tried to put the Cyclops's curse out of my mind, and we sailed on peacefully enough until we reached the island of Aeolus, Keeper of the Winds.

Unlike our last host, Aeolus welcomed us kindly. We stayed at his palace for a month, feasting and telling stories.

When we left, Aeolus gave me a strange and wonderful present.

"Here," he said, handing me a bulging cloth bag. "This bag contains powerful winds. Let out just a few puffs if you need to change course."

I put the bag in a safe place, where my men wouldn't accidentally open it, and we went on our way.

Then Aeolus sent us a steady breeze to blow us home. Before we knew it, we were close enough to Ithaca to see people walking about on the shore. I couldn't wait to get back to my kingdom and to see my family again after all those years.

By now, I was so exhausted that I couldn't keep my eyes open, and I took a nap. I dreamed of Penelope, my darling wife, and Telemachus, my son, who must be almost a man now.

As I slept, some of my men pulled out the bag full of winds. They must have thought it contained treasure or some other precious thing I was trying to keep to myself, because they opened it.

A mighty hurricane whipped up around us. I woke with a start and realized that my men had released all the winds at once.

We were blown back and back and back the way we had come… all the way back to Aeolus. This time, he wouldn't help us.

"The gods seem against you," he said. "I can't do anything more."

So, we set sail yet again, only this time, without the winds of Aeolus, our ships seemed to crawl through the water.

After a while, we came to an island and landed to stock up on food and water.

I spotted a plump girl walking along the road, and I called out to her. She told us to go and see her mother and father, the king and queen of the Laestrygones, in their palace on the hill.

"They'd be delighted to have you for supper," she said, with a smile that I really didn't like.

When we met the king and queen, we quickly discovered why they'd be so delighted to have us for supper — they were cannibals!

We ran for our lives, but not all of us escaped. The Laestrygones soldiers chased us all the way to the shore and hurled rocks at us, smashing almost all of our ships and killing many of my men.

Only one single ship of sad, tired men sailed away from that island. We had no supplies, and hardly any hope left in our hearts.

Next time we landed, I was more cautious. We drew lots, and one group of men stayed at the shore with me, while the other followed Eurylochus to explore and look for food and fresh running water.

The scouting party soon came upon a grand stone house in the woods. Eurylochus told me later that outside the house he saw a group of wolves and lions as meek and friendly as puppies and kittens. One lion even rolled on its back to have its tummy tickled.

A woman was singing somewhere nearby. At the sound of their footsteps, she appeared in the doorway and beckoned. "Come, strangers. You look tired. Let me offer you refreshments."

My weary men went in, hungry and eager and enchanted with this gentle, beautiful stranger.

"Come in, come in," she sang to them. "I am Circe and you are welcome in my home. I have sweet wine, fresh bread and honey and olives, ready and waiting for you."

But Eurylochus stayed behind. We'd had so little good luck on our journeys that he couldn't help thinking she was just a little *too* interested in feeding them.

He peered through the window to see the men stuffing their faces with food.

As they ate, Circe brought them extra little treats
and kept their cups full to overflowing. She smiled at
them and they seemed to be having a wonderful time
– as far as Eurylochus could tell.

Too late, the men discovered that the wine was
drugged. Eurylochus watched them slump into a
deep, deep sleep. Circe waved a slender wand, and
cried out, "Since you eat like pigs... pigs you shall be!"

Each sleeping man transformed into an
oinking, snuffling, pink, wriggling pig.

Eurylochus ran all the way back to me and told me what he'd seen.

Telling him not to let the rest of the men out of his sight, whatever happened, I set off along the path in the direction of the stone house.

Before I'd gone half the distance, a beautiful young man in winged sandals flew down from the sky and handed me a small sprig of magic herbs.

"I am the god Hermes," he said. "Here, eat these herbs. They will protect you from Circe's magic."

Before I could reply, he flew away again.

I swallowed the herbs and went on my way. At the house, I saw the tame wolves and lions and wondered if they, too, had once been men.

Circe welcomed me, offering food and wine. I ate and drank, just as my men had done – but I knew I was safe, thanks to Hermes.

Circe waved her wand, chuckling to herself, no doubt thrilled that she'd found another gullible idiot... but nothing happened. "Why aren't you changing?" she pouted.

"That's my business," I said, and drew my sword. "Now, change my men back!"

Circe looked impressed. "It's been a long time since anyone has been able to cheat my magic." She smiled softly. "Perhaps you would like to stay as my guest instead of my prisoner?"

Her eyes twinkled as she spoke, and in that instant, I began to fall in love. Or perhaps, despite the herb, I was falling under another spell.

Still, I hadn't entirely lost my mind. "I'll only stay if you swear that you don't mean me any harm," I said. "And," I added, "you must reverse the spell you cast on my men before I'll trust you."

Circe sighed, and agreed. "I swear on all the gods that I will do you no harm." Then, she called the pigs – my men, I mean – to her and tapped each one gently on the head with her wand.

The pigs began to change and grow, until my men all stood before me, looking dazed and scared.

I explained that Circe had sworn that she wouldn't hurt us again, so we all decided to stay for a while. I have to admit, it was pleasant to be in a place where no one was trying to kill me or eat me, for a change.

Chapter 5

The land of the dead

After a year on Circe's island, my men grew restless, and I knew deep down that it was time for us to leave.

"If you don't want to stay, I won't stop you," said Circe. "But, take my advice. If you want to get home in one piece, you will have to visit the land of the dead and seek the help of Tiresias, a spirit there."

When she suggested this, I was terrified. "How can we go to the land of the dead and not die?" I asked her. "And how do we even get there?"

Circe reassured me and gave me a long list of instructions, as well as many warnings for our journey beyond the land of the dead. "Let the North Wind carry you," she said as she waved us off in our one remaining ship. "Good luck!"

Soon, we landed on the misty shores of the land of the dead. It was just as eerie and depressing as its name makes it sound.

As Circe had instructed, I dug a hole and poured the blood of a freshly-killed sheep into it. This was to tempt the dead out of the shadows to talk to us. The dead drink blood, you see. It reminds them of life's warmth.

As the blood poured into the hole, shadowy spirits gathered around us. My men trembled, but I tried to keep my voice steady as I called, "Tiresias! Come forward! Odysseus wants to speak to you!"

One shadowy figure drifted closer, bending to take a drink of the blood. As he began to look more solid, I saw he was an old, old man.

"You're in trouble," he said. "Poseidon wants you dead to avenge his son, the Cyclops."

My heart sank. But there was more...

"Whatever you do, stay away from the cattle of Helios, the sun god. If you eat those..." He shook his head. "Just don't."

With the warning ringing in my ears, we left the land of the dead and sailed on. Circe had told me that another danger lay ahead: the sirens.

In case you've never heard of them, sirens are monsters with beautiful voices who lure sailors into the sea, to sleep forever in watery graves.

I gave my men wax to block their ears. But I wanted to hear these voices for myself. So, I got my men to tie me firmly to the mast before we were in earshot of the sirens. Soon, I heard them...

Their voices were high and sweet, caressing my ears and urging me to come nearer, to dive into the sea... I begged my men, "Please, oh please, let me go to them! I have to go to them!"

Thankfully, my men couldn't hear me through their wax ear-plugs. So I may be the first person to hear the sirens and live.

But another danger loomed ahead. Another two, in fact. We had to pass a narrow gap in the rocks. On one side was a whirlpool, created by the sea monster Charybdis.

On the other side was a cave where a six-headed monster lived. Her name was Scylla.

I knew that some of us would not get through alive. "Faster!" I called to the men at the oars. "Don't get too close to the whirlpool, or we'll all drown!"

Just then, Scylla whipped her heads out of her cave above us. The six heads snatched up six of my men in their greedy mouths.

But the rest of us were through the gap and sailing on, safe again for the moment.

Chapter 6

The cattle of the sun

We stopped for the night on an island full of golden cattle. Seeing their shining skins, I guessed that they were the cattle of the sun god, Helios, that Tiresias had warned me about.

I addressed my men in my sternest voice. "Whatever you do, do NOT eat these cattle. Don't even look at them."

For a while, the men obeyed. But we were running low on food and my men began to mutter: "If we starve, we'll be dead anyway."

The next day, I jolted awake to the smell of roasting meat. My men were eating the cattle.

"Fools!" I cried. But it was too late — the damage was done. With a heavy heart, I ushered everyone back onto the ship and we set sail. What else could we do but press on?

Moments later, the sun god Helios smashed
our boat into little tiny pieces.
I was the only survivor.

I found myself shipwrecked on an island, where I was taken prisoner by a magical woman named Calypso. I spent seven long years there, pining for home, until the great god Zeus sent a messenger to free me. And so here I am...

Chapter 7

Ithaca at last

As soon as Odysseus had finished his tale, he fell fast asleep right there on the throne room floor. The king ordered his guards to take poor Odysseus home at once. Still fast asleep, Odysseus was carried on board a ship.

When he awoke, he was on the shore of a land he thought he recognized.

With tears in his eyes, he realized: "It's Ithaca!" He kissed the ground with joy.

At that moment, a tall, beautiful woman appeared. She was wearing a breastplate that glinted in the dawn light, and had a shining helmet upon her head. It was Athena, Goddess of Wisdom. She had been watching over Odysseus all this time.

"Welcome home, at long last," said the goddess. "But before you can claim your kingdom, you have one last job to do... and you must do it in disguise."

With a sweeping wave of her hand, she transformed Odysseus into a ragged old beggar.

Odysseus gazed at his newly-wrinkled hands in shock. But he still had his wits about him. "What's the job?" he asked. "I'll do whatever you want."

"While you've been away, your house has been full of scroungers," said Athena. "They've been eating your food and making your family's life a misery. You must defeat them before you claim your wife. You see, they hope that one of them can marry her."

326

"But she *is* married!" cried Odysseus. "To me!"

"You've been gone a long time – Penelope's suitors think you're dead," said Athena. "But I can help you get rid of them. Go and rest in the cottage on the hill. It belongs to Eumaeus the shepherd. He's always been loyal to you."

With that, she disappeared.

Eumaeus welcomed the strange old man and offered him a place by the fire. Odysseus played the part of a feeble old beggar so convincingly that the kindly shepherd insisted that Odysseus take his own soft bed that night while he slept outside.

The next morning, Odysseus was awoken by Athena. She was smiling, and she said, "I have someone to see you. But first..." She waved her hands and he felt his old and wrinkled skin become firmer and younger again.

Just then, a young man appeared over the crest of the hill. He looked familiar. Very familiar.

"Telemachus!" Odysseus cried. "My son!" He rushed forward to hug him.

Telemachus jumped back in shock. Odysseus's skin was still glowing from the transformation, and he looked more like a god than a man.

"Telemachus, I'm your father," said Odysseus. "Don't you recognize me?"

Telemachus's shock turned to joy, and he flung his arms around his father.

"It's time," said a voice from behind them. They turned to see Athena. "Go and reclaim your kingdom from those disgraceful men who are bleeding it dry," she said. Her eyes were stern.

Once again, she disguised Odysseus as a beggar. "You'll have the advantage of surprise," she said.

So, the old Odysseus and young Telemachus walked to town, picking up Eumaeus on their way.

As they drew close to the city walls, a dog
bounded up to Odysseus – an ancient thing, all
matted hair and creaky limbs. It was Odysseus's
own dog, that he'd left behind as a puppy. "Good
boy, good boy!" beamed Odysseus. But his smile
faded as he realized that the ancient creature was
on its last legs. "Poor boy," he whispered, kneeling
to pet the dog as tears rolled down his cheeks.

But then Odysseus stood, and all the pent-up rage and bitterness of his long, long exile turned into grim determination. He would get his kingdom back and live happily ever after with his wife and son, if he had to kill everyone on the face of the planet to do it.

Chapter 8
The challenge

When they arrived at the palace, things were just as Athena had said. The great hall was full of men lazing around, eating and drinking, ordering Odysseus's servants to bring them the finest things in the kitchen. Odysseus had to restrain himself from killing them all on the spot.

Then he saw her: Penelope, his beloved wife. Wrinkles marked the corners of her eyes, but he thought she was the most beautiful woman he'd ever seen. He was bursting to kiss her, but he thought: *"Steady, Odysseus. You have to get rid of these suitors before you can claim your wife again."*

Penelope saw him — or rather, she saw a ragged beggar. She called for her maid to take care of him. "Welcome, stranger. Please, rest a while." She looked around at the suitors with a wry smile. "Everyone else is making themselves at home, after all."

Odysseus followed the old maid upstairs, where she prepared a bowl of hot water to bathe his feet. As she did so, he realized he knew her – she was the maid who had taken care of him when he was a baby, so many years ago.

"There, that's better," she said, gently rubbing his feet and legs. All of a sudden, she stopped. "That scar on your knee looks awfully familiar. My master has one just like it... Master?" she gasped.

She put a hand up to his face and stroked it gently. "How is it possible? You're so old."

Odysseus grinned and put a finger to his lips. "Shh! Everything will be revealed in time. Don't ruin my surprise!"

When Odysseus went downstairs, he saw Penelope walk into the middle of the great hall carrying a giant hunting bow.

That's my bow, Odysseus thought.

Behind Penelope trooped servants, carrying axes.

"I have decided," she said. "It's been long enough. Odysseus must be dead... and I will marry whoever can string this bow and shoot an arrow through those axes to hit the wooden target."

All the suitors rushed forward, each one convinced that he would be able to do it easily. Each one tried. Each one failed.

"Let me try," said Odysseus, at last.

The suitors yelled insults, but Penelope hushed them and Odysseus took the bow. He bent it, strung it and fired an arrow, in the time it takes to blink.

As the arrow hit the wooden target with a loud *THUNK*, everyone in the room gasped.

"Who ARE you?" said Penelope. She peered at his wrinkled face. "Do I know you from somewhere?"

Odysseus nodded. He took her hand and kissed it, then turned to address the whole room. "I am King Odysseus!" he said. "And I'm here to claim my kingdom and my wife!"

The suitors roared in confusion and anger. Odysseus strung his bow once more and fired it into the crowd of suitors.

Telemachus and Eumaeus — who was looking very surprised indeed — backed him up, armed with spears that Telemachus had hidden earlier.

The suitors howled, "Two old men, and a boy who barely needs to shave, against all of us? We'll slaughter you!" But, as they attacked, they found that none of their blows hit home.

In the corner, the goddess Athena watched quietly. Each time the suitors tried to strike, she made a gesture that sent their weapons glancing off target.

The battle was over almost before it began. Odysseus and his army of two were victorious. Athena touched his forehead, and the old beggar became a mighty king once more.

Penelope stared at him in shock... which turned into suspicion. "Sir. You do *look* like my husband, but since you were an old man five minutes ago, I don't know who or what you really are. Still, since you passed my test, I will marry you tomorrow." But secretly, she decided to set this man another little test. "I'll have my marriage bed brought down here so you can sleep in luxury tonight," she said.

Odysseus was confused. "You can't do that!" he objected. "Our bed is carved out of a living tree so it can't be moved from our bedroom!"

At that, Penelope burst into tears of joy. "Odysseus, it's really you!" she cried, and threw her arms around him.

For a second, Odysseus was stunned, but then he grinned. "My clever Penelope, you were just testing me, weren't you?"

Penelope smiled through her tears. "Yes. But now I have my own Odysseus home at last."

"Home at last," sighed Odysseus, in delight.

More myths
and a guide to the gods

The myths in this collection are just six of many tales told in Ancient Greece thousands of years ago. Some, such as the first myth below describing how the world began, were the Ancient Greeks' way of understanding their world. Other myths, of heroes battling monsters helped (or hindered) by the gods, may have been based on real people and events.

This section has summaries of several more myths, followed by a guide to the gods, and a map showing where much of the action took place.

In the beginning

At first, there was nothing, which the Greeks named Chaos. But out of Chaos, the universe was born.

The very first being to appear was Gaia, or Mother Earth. Shortly after Gaia, Uranus, Lord of the Sky burst into existence. Together, Gaia and Uranus had dozens of children, including the immense Titans; the massive, one-eyed Cyclops; and the Hundred-handers, giants with one hundred hands and fifty heads each.

Their most famous child was Cronus, a Titan who overthrew his father and ruled the world with his brothers and sisters. His son, Zeus, overthrew him in turn and became King of the Gods.

Pandora's box

Once the world was a perfectly happy place. Then a Titan named Prometheus showed humans how to make fire and Zeus, having punished him, decided to punish humans as well. So he ordered his son to create a woman out of clay and named her Pandora.

Zeus gave Pandora a wonderful box but told her she could never, ever open it. One day, Pandora's curiosity grew too much. Slowly, she lifted the lid. In a frenzy, out flew all the things that make the world miserable: sins, sickness, war and death.

As Pandora watched, appalled, one last thing fluttered out: hope. From that day on, life on earth was never easy, but no matter how hard things became, people always had hope.

How the seasons came to be

Persephone, daughter of Demeter, the Goddess of
Nature, was so beautiful that Hades, the King of the
Underworld, fell in love with her and whisked her off
to live with him in his underground palace.

Demeter was devastated. She abandoned everything
to rescue her daughter: the world grew cold and
plants withered and died. Finally, it was agreed that
Persephone would spend only half the year with Hades,
which is when earth is plunged into winter. For the rest
of the year, Persephone moves in with her mother, the
sun shines and crops grow.

Jason and the Golden Fleece

Jason — rightful heir to the throne of Iolcus — was
cast aside by Pelias, his wicked uncle. Pelias then
sent Jason on an almost impossible quest hoping
he wouldn't return. He ordered Jason to bring
him the Golden Fleece, a sheepskin which
hung on a tree far away in Colchis, and was

guarded by a dragon that never slept.

Jason set sail on a ship named the *Argo*, along with his crew, the Argonauts. When at last they arrived in Colchis, the king, Aeetes, set Jason three tasks: to yoke himself to fire-breathing oxen and sow a field with dragon's teeth; to defeat the army of warriors which sprang up from the teeth; and then to overcome the sleepless dragon. Luckily for Jason, the gods made the king's daughter, Medea, fall in love with him and, with her help, Jason successfully completed all three tasks.

Paris and the Beauty Contest

The Trojan War, finally won thanks to a trick with a wooden horse, all began with a beauty contest. Three goddesses couldn't agree who was the fairest so they asked the Trojan prince, Paris, to judge. He chose Aphrodite, who promised him the most beautiful girl in the world as his wife. Unfortunately, this was Helen who was already married — to Menelaus, the King of Sparta. Paris stole Helen away, infuriating the Spartans and triggering the war.

Achilles

Achilles was the son of a goddess and a mortal. His mother tried to make him invincible by burning his mortal side away in a fire. But she held onto his heel, which was left unprotected. It was on exactly this spot that he was killed, by an arrow fired by Paris during the Trojan War.

Icarus and Daedalus

Daedalus was a great inventor, who designed the labyrinth on Crete to house the monstrous Minotaur. Then he fell out with King Minos and had to flee. He and his son Icarus flew to freedom on wings they made themselves out of wax and feathers. But Icarus ignored his father's warnings to stay away from the sun. Instead, Icarus soared as high as he could. The wax melted, his wings fell apart and Icarus plummeted into the sea and was drowned.

Gods and goddesses – a guide

The gods lived in a grand palace high in the clouds, above Greece's tallest mountain, Mount Olympus. Each one had special powers and all were immortal, which meant they could live forever.

Zeus: ruler of the universe, he watched over the world and the humans below, sometimes interfering in their lives. The Cyclops gave him a set of thunderbolts, which he threw when he was angry.

Hera: Zeus's wife, protector of women and marriage, beautiful but proud and jealous.

Poseidon: ruler of the seas, nick-named "Earth-shaker" because the Greeks believed he caused earthquakes. He carried a trident (three-pronged fork), which he used to whip up storms.

Hades: god of the Underworld and ruler of the dead, he owned all the precious metals and gems buried in the earth.

Hestia: goddess of the hearth and home.

Demeter: goddess of plants and nature.

Ares: son of Zeus and Hera and god of war.

Hephaistos: brother of Ares, he was a blacksmith, and patron of craftsmen. His forge stood beneath the volcanic Mount Etna on the island of Sicily.

Aphrodite: goddess of love and beauty, she was married to Hephaistos but in love with Ares.

Athena: daughter of Zeus and Metis (a Titan), the goddess of wisdom and war. She sprang from Zeus's head fully grown and fully armed.

Artemis: goddess of the moon and hunting.

Apollo: twin brother of Artemis, he was god of the sun, light, truth and music. He had a shrine at Delphi, where Greeks would go to ask his advice.

Hermes: messenger to the gods.

Dionysus: god of wine and fertility.

Eros: god of love, the son of Ares and Aphrodite. His magical arrows could make humans fall in love.

A note about names

The Romans, who rose to power after the Greeks, adopted many Greek gods but gave them new names — often, the names they are known by today. Here, the Greek names are followed by the Roman ones.

Aphrodite ~ Venus

Apollo ~ Apollo

Artemis ~ Diana

Ares ~ Mars

Athena ~ Minerva

Demeter ~ Ceres

Dionysus ~ Bacchus

Eros ~ Cupid

Hades ~ Pluto

Hephaistos ~ Vulcan

Hera ~ Juno

Hermes ~ Mercury

Hestia ~ Vesta

Poseidon ~ Neptune

Zeus ~ Jupiter

Map of Ancient Greece

MACEDONIA

THRACE

Heracles bound the man-eating mares here.

Heracles went this way to find the island of the Amazons.

Mount Olympus

Troy

The Wooden Horse

THESSALY

AEGEAN SEA

Ceryneian Deer

Erymanthian Boar

Delphi

Mount Helicon

Bellerophon found Pegasus here.

Nemean Lion

Mount Erymanthus

Ceryneia

Athens

Icarus

ICARIAN SEA

Ithaca, home of Odysseus

Nemea

Stymphalis

Tiryns

ELIS

Lerna

Heracles cleaned the stables of King Augeas of Elis.

Naxos

Heracles slew the hydra that lived near Lerna.

Sparta

Heracles defeated the birds plaguing Stymphalis.

The Minotaur, slain by Theseus

Cape Taenarum

Heracles tamed the fire-breathing bull here.

IONIAN SEA

Heracles entered the Underworld here to capture Cerberus.

Heracles went this way in search of Geryon and the Hesperides.

CRETE

Knossos

Usborne Quicklinks

For a pronunciation guide to the Greek names in this book, and links to websites where you can find out more about Greek myths and life in Ancient Greece, go to www.usborne.com/quicklinks and enter the keywords 'Illustrated Greek Myths'.

When using the internet please follow the internet safety guidelines displayed on the Usborne Quicklinks website. The recommended websites in Usborne Quicklinks are regularly reviewed and updated, but Usborne Publishing Ltd. is not responsible for the content or availability of any website other than its own. We recommend that children are supervised while using the internet.

History consultant: Dr. Anne Millard

Designed by Michelle Lawrence and Emily Bornoff
Cover design: Louise Flutter
Digital design: Nick Wakeford

First published in 2011 by Usborne Publishing Ltd,
83-85 Saffron Hill, London EC1N 8RT, England.
www.usborne.com Copyright © 2011 Usborne Publishing Ltd.
First published in America in 2012 U.E.